Paw and Order

Max was concentrating intently on the basement door. Then he started whining and scrabbling away at the bottom of it. Every muscle in his strong, lean body tensed as he tried with all his might to get it open.

Then the twins froze. A loud, scratching noise was coming from the basement, right underneath their feet.

Now they knew why Max was making such a fuss.

PAW AND ORDER

Jenny Dale

Illustrated by Mick Reid

A
LITTLE APPLE
PAPERBACK

SCHOLASTIC INC.

New York Toronto London Auckland Sydney
Mexico City New Delhi Hong Kong Buenos Aires

ISBN 0-439-32262-6

12 11 10 9 8 7 6 5   3 4 5 6/0

Printed in the U.S.A.   40

First Scholastic printing, September 2001

Special thanks to Narinder Dhami.

Many thanks also to
Steve Dean and Peter Whitehead
of the Metropolitan Police Service for their
invaluable advice.

In memory of Metpol Bruno 40 —
who served as a fine police dog for ten years.

Chapter One

"This is cool!" said ten-year-old Liam Wilson. He stood in the empty bedroom, looking around with a big grin on his face. The room was large and airy, and it looked out over the main street of the town and the hills of the Peak District beyond.

As Liam stared out the window, two boys zoomed past on mountain bikes. A large crowd was playing football in the park and having a great time by the look of it. Liam's grin grew even wider. Ellandale was so different from the city he and his family had just left. He was going to *love* living here.

Liam spun around as his twin sister, Becky, burst into the room along with Max, the Wilsons' German shepherd dog. "I want this room," he said quickly.

"Hey, that's not fair!" Becky grumbled, pushing her long, dark hair from her face. "Mom said we had to decide together!"

"Well, I was here first!" Liam argued, making a face at his sister. "Wasn't I, Max?"

Max cocked his head to one side and stared solemnly from Becky to Liam with big dark eyes as if he understood perfectly what they were saying.

"Typical!" Becky grumbled, but Liam could tell that she was too excited to be really annoyed. He followed her out and into the back bedroom.

"Oh, this is great!" Becky exclaimed, her face brightening. Although the room was smaller than Liam's, it had a fantastic view. Lark Cottage had fields behind it, stretching as far as the eye could see, and a winding river that glittered in the morning sun.

"Maybe I'll take this one instead!" Liam remarked wickedly.

Becky gave him a shove. "You're a pain, Liam Wilson!" she snorted.

Meanwhile, Max was sniffing around in the corner of the room, investigating the scents left behind by the previous owners. His long tail swished from side to side.

Becky crouched down beside him and

stroked his silky ears. "You look at home already, don't you, Max?" She grinned. "I think he's going to like it here!"

"So are we!" Liam said confidently. He didn't have to ask if Becky agreed with him. They were so close that they could almost always guess what the other was thinking. They'd been shocked when their father, John Wilson, a policeman, told them he had a new job and they would have to move. But as soon as they'd set eyes on the town of Ellandale in the Derbyshire Dales, they'd begun to change their minds.

Becky ruffled the German shepherd's thick black-and-brown fur. "Max starts work with Dad tomorrow, doesn't he?"

Liam nodded. "Yes, so all the crooks in Ellandale had better watch out!" he joked, sliding an arm around Max's neck.

Max woofed and thumped his tail against the bare floor.

The German shepherd was no ordinary family pet. He was a highly trained police dog, and the twins' father was his handler. Max had come to live with the Wilsons when he was just twelve weeks old and had quickly become one of the family. Now that he had completed his long training course, he would be helping Officer Wilson fight crime in his new job around Ellandale.

Max's tail stopped wagging. His ears pricked up and he listened, an alert expression on his face.

A second later the voice of the twins' mother, Tina Wilson, floated up the stairs. "Have you two decided which bedrooms you want yet?"

Liam and Becky both smiled. Even though they were used to Max's amazing ability to stay alert to every sight or sound, it never failed to impress them. The fact that nothing escapes the attention of a German shepherd was one of

the reasons why they were in such de-
mand as police dogs.

"Yes, Liam wants the front and I want
the back!" Becky called.

"Good," said Mrs. Wilson, coming
into the room. She pushed back a lock of
fair hair with a dusty hand. She was a
nurse and could usually be relied on to
be supercool and efficient, but today the
stress of moving was clearly beginning
to get to her. "Now, will you come
downstairs so that the moving men can
bring the furniture up, please?"

Becky, Liam, and Max clattered downstairs as John Wilson came in through
the door with yet another large box.

"All right, you two?" he asked with a
smile. A tall, well-built man, he seemed
very laid-back, but he had an air of calm
authority about him.

They both nodded enthusiastically.

"Hey, let's go and check out the backyard!" Becky said, nudging Liam in the ribs, and they ran off down the hallway, Max bounding along beside them.

With its stone floor, old pine cupboards, and open fireplace at one end, the kitchen was very different from the modern one in their city house. In fact, the whole cottage, with its slightly sloping walls, winding corridors, and exposed beams was totally different from the modern house they had left behind.

"Look." Liam pointed at the back door, which leaned slightly to the left. "It's all crooked!"

"So's this one." Becky stared at a large wooden door in the corner of the kitchen. "I wonder where it goes?"

"Dad said the basement is down

there," Liam told her. "How old do you think the house is?"

"Didn't you see the carved stone over the door when we came in?" Becky asked. She always noticed details like that. "It says Lark Cottage, 1820."

"1820!" Liam was impressed. Then he grinned. "I wonder if it has a ghost!"

Becky shook her head. "Of course not," she said quickly, not liking the idea very much. "Anyway," she added, "if there *are* any ghosts, Max will soon catch them!"

"Max can be our official ghost-catcher!" Liam joked. He glanced down at the dog and then frowned. "Hey, what's wrong with him?"

Max was concentrating intently on the basement door. Then he started whining and scrabbling away at the

9

bottom of it, and every muscle in his strong, lean body tensed as he tried with all his might to get it open.

"Maybe he's found a ghost already!" Becky joked back.

Then the twins froze. A loud, scratching noise was coming from the basement, right underneath their feet.

Now they knew why Max was making such a fuss.

Chapter Two

Liam and Becky grabbed each other in fright. Meanwhile, Max redoubled his efforts to get the door open.

"What was *that*?" Liam whispered, his eyes wide.

"Maybe it's a mouse," Becky hissed.

"It'd have to be as big as Max to make that kind of noise!" Liam replied.

They looked at each other.

"Maybe it *is* a ghost!" Liam muttered.

"Don't be silly," Becky said stoutly.

"We'll just have to go and see for ourselves!" Liam said, reaching for the key that hung on a hook on the wall.

"Maybe we should go and tell Mom and Dad," Becky suggested nervously. Liam was always rushing into situations like this, and it had gotten them both into trouble more than once.

"We'll take Max," Liam said. "You know he'll look after us."

Becky nodded. Max was fiercely protective of them both and would never let anything hurt them.

As Liam cautiously pushed the door open, they heard the scratching noise again. This time it was louder.

"Sit, Max!" Becky said sharply as Max attempted to dash down the stairs.

Max immediately sat. His whole body was still, but alert, and his ears were cocked.

Liam took a firm hold of Max's collar. "Okay," he said bravely, "shall we go down?"

"Isn't there a light or something?" Becky asked, peering over Liam's shoulder into the pitch-black, musty darkness.

Liam felt along the wall and flipped a switch. A dim light came on, but it wasn't really bright enough to light up the whole basement, which ran the length of the house.

Slowly, Liam began to walk down the stairs, Max pressed close against him and Becky following behind.

They were halfway down when they heard the scratching noise again.

"It's coming from over there!" Becky whispered, pointing to some boxes in the corner. Max was already straining to go in that direction.

Liam let go of Max's collar, and he bounded down the steps, barking loudly. An answering woof made Liam and Becky glance at each other in surprise. The next moment, a little brown-and-white Jack Russell terrier popped out of one of the boxes and barked at them, its stumpy tail wagging.

"It's a dog!" Liam exclaimed.

"Oh, what a shame!" Becky grinned. "I was really looking forward to meeting the ghost of Lark Cottage!"

The dog scrambled out of the box, and he and Max introduced themselves by sniffing cautiously at each other. Then the dog ran over to Liam and Becky and danced around their ankles, barking merrily while they stroked him.

"I wonder where he came from," Liam said, laughing as the overexcited terrier ran around in circles trying to catch its own tail. "Do you think he's a stray?"

Becky shook her head. "He's wearing a tag." She bent down and picked the Jack Russell up. But it was hard to read the tag while he was enthusiastically giving her face a good wash. "Stop it!"

Becky giggled. "Come on, we'd better go and tell Mom and Dad."

"Becky! Liam!" Right at that moment they heard their mother's voice overhead in the kitchen. "What on earth are you doing in the basement?"

"You'll never guess!" Becky called back as they all hurried upstairs.

As they came out into the kitchen, Tina Wilson turned to them with a smile. She had two people with her, a fair-haired woman carrying a delicious-smelling pie and a girl of about the same age as the twins, who also had fair hair. "Becky, Liam, I want you to meet our new neighbors. This is Mrs. Gibbs and her daughter, Julie." Then she stopped, her eyes widening. "Where on *earth* did that dog come from?"

"Well —" Becky began, but she didn't get a chance to say anything more.

Julie saw the dog in Becky's arms and rushed over. "Scooter, you naughty boy! I've been looking for you everywhere!"

Scooter yapped joyfully as Julie took him from Becky.

"Is he yours?" Liam asked. "He was in our basement."

"So that's where he's been going!" Julie exclaimed.

"Our basement runs alongside yours, so there must be a hole in the wall somewhere," Julie's mother said. "I'll get my husband to check and block it up."

"We thought it was a ghost!" Becky grinned.

"No, it was just Scooter's way of

welcoming you to Ellandale!" Julie laughed.

"And that's why we're here, too, even though Scooter got in ahead of us!" Mrs. Gibbs handed Tina Wilson the pie plate. "I was doing some baking and thought you might appreciate an apple pie."

"How kind!" Mrs. Wilson said gratefully. "It smells delicious. That's dessert taken care of for later!"

"Is this your dog?" Julie asked the twins, looking down at Max who was sitting quietly next to them. "He's beautiful."

"Yes, Max is a really special dog," Liam said proudly. "He works with our dad. He's a policeman."

"I know," Julie said. "Everyone in town knows about Max. We were told about it at the Neighborhood Watch meeting. We're all really excited!"

"Did you hear that, Max?" Becky said, patting the German shepherd's head. Max nuzzled her hand with his cold black nose. "You're famous already!"

"Maybe your dad could give me a few tips on how to train Scooter!" Julie sighed, struggling to prevent the terrier from chewing the neck of her T-shirt. "Are you starting at Ellandale Elementary School tomorrow?"

Liam nodded. "We're in fourth grade — Ms. Kendall's class."

Julie's face lit up. "So am I!"

"Oh, great!" Becky was pleased, too. She already liked Julie a lot. "What's Ms. Kendall like?"

"Oh, she's cool!" Julie assured them.

"She's a little strict, but she can be funny, too."

"Come on, Julie." Mrs. Gibbs said to her daughter. "Let's get out of our new neighbors' way so that they can finish their unpacking."

"Okay, Mom." Julie grinned at Liam and Becky. "See you tomorrow!"

"Well, that's our first friend in Ellandale," Becky said happily as Julie and her mother went home.

Liam nodded. "And it looks like Max has made a friend, too," he said as Max watched Scooter go next door. "Is it time for lunch yet, Mom?" he asked.

Mrs. Wilson groaned. "I can't even think about cooking at the moment! Why don't you take Max for a quick walk along the road, and then we'll send your dad for takeout?"

"Great!" The twins rushed to get Max's leash, and soon they were unlatching the gate at the end of the long, overgrown yard. After living in London, where the view from their yard was another row of houses, it was odd now to see a field with woodlands beyond.

"Don't be too long, and stay where I can see you from the house!" their mother called.

"Mom never liked us taking Max out for walks on our own when we lived in London," Becky remarked.

"Well, the country's different, isn't it?" Liam replied. "There's not so much traffic, for one thing. It's a lot safer."

Becky sighed happily. "It's going to be great living here! Everyone's so friendly —" She broke off suddenly as

Max stopped dead in his tracks and stiffened.

Liam stared down at him. "What's wrong, boy?" he asked.

Max was staring at a large clump of bushes. Every hair on his body seemed to bristle with tension as he stood still as a stone.

"There's something in those bushes!" Becky whispered urgently.

"Is someone there?" Liam called, trying not to sound nervous. "If there is, you'd better come out now!"

There was a rustling in the bushes, and Liam and Becky tensed as Max growled. Who — or what — had he found this time?

Chapter Three

A second later, the bushes parted, and a boy stepped out. He had tousled brown hair and wore old jeans and a baggy T-shirt.

Liam and Becky stared at him.

"You nearly scared us to death!" Becky cried.

"Sorry," the boy muttered, keeping a wary eye on Max.

"It's okay, he won't hurt you," Liam said quickly. "He was just trying to protect us. It's all right, Max. Friend." He looked at the boy. "Just hold out your hand so he can get your scent." German shepherd dogs are usually suspicious of strangers, which is another of the reasons why they make such good police dogs.

The boy did as Liam said. Max sniffed at him with interest, accepted that the boy was no danger to Liam and Becky, and sat down quietly on his haunches.

"What were you doing in the bushes?" Becky asked curiously.

"Nothing," the boy muttered. "I lost something, that's all."

Liam thought that was a pretty lame excuse, but he didn't get a chance to say anything as Becky chimed in again.

"What's your name? How old are you? Do you live in Ellandale?" she quizzed.

The boy looked down at his feet. "I'm Paul, and I'm ten. We've just moved to Ellandale."

"So have we!" Becky exclaimed, delighted. "I'm Becky, and this is my twin brother, Liam. You must be going to Ellandale Elementary School, too. Are you in Ms. Kendall's class?"

"Er — maybe . . ." Paul muttered.

Liam wondered why Paul looked so

uncomfortable, although he was trying to hide it by stroking Max.

Paul noticed Liam staring at him and blushed. "I've got a dog, too," he muttered.

"Oh, what's its name?" Becky asked with interest. "And what kind is it?"

Paul shrugged. "He's a mutt named Bouncer."

"You'll have to bring him over to meet Max," Becky said happily. "Then we can all go out for walks!"

"I can't!" Paul said quickly. Then he added, "I mean, Bouncer's staying with . . . someone else at the moment — until we've settled in."

Liam wondered why Paul looked so miserable when he said that. Maybe it was just because he missed his dog so much. Liam couldn't help feeling sorry for him. "I bet you miss him. Why don't you walk home with us and Max — you can stay for lunch if you want," he suggested.

Paul's face lit up. "Could I?"

"Sure!" Liam said. "Mom won't mind — but perhaps you need to tell yours?"

Paul shook his head quickly. "No . . . my mom won't mind, either," he mumbled.

"Great!" Liam beamed. "Come on!"

Becky secretly thought their mother might mind since she was so busy, but there was no stopping Liam once he got an idea into his head.

As they headed back to the cottage, Liam couldn't help noticing that Paul didn't say very much, but he really seemed to like being with Max. Maybe he was just shy — and missing his own dog.

"Hi, you all." Their father was in the kitchen putting on his jacket when they arrived home. "I'm just off to get pizzas." He smiled at Paul. "Who's this?"

"Paul," Paul muttered, shuffling his feet.

John Wilson raised an eyebrow at him and eventually the boy added, "Carter. Paul Carter."

"He's just moved to Ellandale, and Liam's invited him for lunch," Becky informed her father as her mother hurried into the kitchen.

"Getting into friendly country ways already, are we?" her father teased as he went out.

"So where do you live, Paul?" Tina Wilson asked as she hunted around in one of the cardboard boxes for plates. "Becky, can you find some glasses?"

"Oh, over on the other side of Ellandale," Paul said vaguely.

"Where exactly?" But Tina didn't wait for an answer. "Try that box over there, Becky. I'll be so glad when we've finally got everything organized!"

"What do your mom and dad do, Paul?" Becky asked.

Liam noticed that Paul turned a little red at the question.

"My dad's a journalist," he said reluctantly. "Mom's an accountant."

"Maybe we can meet them tomorrow," Mrs. Wilson suggested, putting a bottle of lemonade on the table.

Paul didn't answer, and Liam could see that he looked relieved when Becky began to chatter on about how great Ellandale was. He plunked himself down next to Max and sat gently ruffling the German shepherd's fur.

"Oh, good — food at last!" said Tina Wilson when the front door slammed shut twenty minutes later.

"Here we are," Officer Wilson said, hurrying into the kitchen with a stack of pizza boxes. "And I've brought someone to meet you all." He turned to smile at the young policewoman who came into the room behind him. "This is Officer Janie Blake. She's going to be working with me at the station."

"Hi, everyone," Janie said. She had bright red hair and a wide smile and looked very friendly.

But as everyone said hello, Liam glanced at Paul. All the color had drained out of his face.

"And this must be Max!" Janie went over to the German shepherd, who was lying under the table, resting his head on Becky's feet. Once he had sniffed at Janie and checked her over, Max wagged his tail and allowed her to stroke him.

"Do you have any pets?" Becky asked.

Janie grinned at her. "Well . . . only my snake, Copper!"

"A snake!" Becky's eyes widened.

"You can come over and see him if you like," Janie told her.

"Would you like to join us for lunch, Janie?" Mrs. Wilson was busy cutting up the pizzas. "We've certainly got enough!"

"I'd love to," Janie replied, "but I'm on duty. I just happened to meet John on my beat." Reluctantly, she went over to the door. "If Jim finds out I'm not working, he won't be too pleased!"

"That's Sergeant Jim Thornton," the twins' father explained. "He's the desk sergeant at the station, so he's based there most of the time."

"She's nice," Becky said after Janie

said her good-byes and left. "But then, *everyone*'s nice here!"

"I hope not!" Liam snorted. "Or Dad and Max won't have much to do!"

Becky made a face. "What's Sergeant Thornton like?" she asked.

"Oh, I hear he's a good police officer," their father replied, picking up a large slice of pizza. "But I think it's going to take a bit of time for him to get used to Max!"

A few moments later, Liam glanced across at Paul again and could hardly believe his eyes. The others had barely started, but Paul had finished his first slice of pizza and was already reaching for a second one. It was as though he hadn't eaten for days.

When Paul had demolished a fourth

slice, he hurriedly pushed his plate away. "Thanks, Mrs. Wilson, that was great," he said. "I've got to go now."

"Don't you want to stay and have some apple pie?" Becky asked. "Our neighbor, Mrs. Gibbs, made it."

Paul hesitated.

"Yes, stay," Mrs. Wilson urged. "You still haven't told us much about your parents or where you live."

Paul looked uncomfortable again. "Sorry, I can't," he said abruptly. "Thanks again. 'Bye." He hurried over to the back door and was gone.

"Well!" Becky sniffed. "That wasn't very friendly, was it?"

"Poor boy. Maybe he's got some problems at home." Mrs. Wilson frowned, then turned to her husband. "John, we'd better get on with the unpacking."

"There's something funny going on with Paul," Liam whispered to Becky.

Becky nodded. "He didn't seem to want to tell us much about himself, did he?"

"And then when Janie came in, he looked really scared, like he'd seen a ghost!" Liam added.

Becky frowned. "I wonder why? Do you think he's in some sort of trouble?"

"I don't know," Liam shrugged. "But maybe we can find out at school tomorrow."

Chapter Four

"I wonder how Max is doing," Liam said as he slung his schoolbag over his shoulder. "After all, it's *his* first day, too!"

It was the next morning, and the twins were walking to school with Julie. Officer Wilson and Max were working the early shift and had left before Liam and Becky had gotten out of bed.

"Max will be fine!" Becky said as the three of them walked across the park. "Isn't it a lovely day?"

The sun was shining again, and the ducks were splashing around in the pond. In the distance they could see the hills of the Peak District, shrouded in a thin mist.

"Wait until the winter," Julie told them. "We usually get snowed in. Once we couldn't get to school for three days!"

"Cool!" Liam said as they arrived at school.

Liam and Becky had visited Ellandale Elementary School at the end of the term so they had already seen the old Victorian building with its red-tiled roof. It was very different from their old school, which was modern.

"I wonder how all our old schoolfriends are," Becky said as they walked through the playground gates. "We could e-mail some of them this weekend."

Liam wasn't listening. He'd just spotted something very interesting going on across the playground. "Hey, Becky, look! There's Max — and Dad, too!"

Sure enough, at the far end of the playground stood Max and Officer Wilson. The twins' father was deep in conversation with a tall, dark-haired woman who wore silver-framed glasses.

Becky recognized her as Mrs. Mason, the principal, whom they'd met when they'd looked around the school. "What on *earth* are they doing here?" she asked, puzzled.

"Well, there's only one way to find out!" Liam raced off across the playground. Becky and Julie followed.

Max had already spotted the twins in the distance, but because he was on duty, he showed no reaction, apart from wagging his tail very slightly.

". . . and we'll certainly do our best to get to the bottom of this," Officer Wilson was saying. Then he smiled. "Hello, you two. I thought we might see you this morning."

"Hi, Dad, what's going on?" Liam asked breathlessly. He and Becky didn't touch Max. They knew better than to do that while he was on duty.

"Good morning, Rebecca and Liam," Mrs. Mason said pointedly. "Welcome to Ellandale Elementary."

Liam blushed. "Good morning, Mrs. Mason," he muttered.

"Good morning, Mrs. Mason," Becky said. But she couldn't help grinning. Not many people managed to put Liam off when he was determined to find out what was going on!

Officer Wilson glanced at the principal. "You did say that you were going to tell the pupils about the thefts, didn't you, Mrs. Mason?"

Mrs. Mason nodded. "Yes, in assembly this morning."

"Well, there's no harm in you three knowing, then," Officer Wilson went on. "It seems that some food that was recently delivered to the school has been stolen."

"What kind of food?" Liam asked.

"Cookies and milk for the teachers' lounge and potato chips and chocolate for the school store," Mrs. Mason said grimly. "They disappeared while the delivery man was unpacking his van in the playground."

"So Max and I are here to investigate," Officer Wilson explained.

"Well, I hope you find out who took them," said Mrs. Mason as she glanced at her watch. "I must go. School starts in five minutes." She turned to leave, then stopped. "Perhaps you and Max would like to come to an assembly sometime and talk to our pupils?" Mrs. Mason glanced at the large crowd of children

41

who were gathering to stare at the dog. "I know they'd be very interested!"

"We'd love to," Officer Wilson said, smiling. "How about Wednesday?"

Mrs. Mason nodded, then hurried off.

The crowd of children edged forward for a closer look at Ellandale's new police dog. Max sat obediently next to his handler, not letting his noisy audience distract him. Liam and Becky grinned at each other. Max always attracted attention wherever he went!

"Can we say good-bye to Max, Dad?" Becky asked as the bell rang for the start of the school day. Her father nodded.

As the twins knelt down to fuss over Max, the German shepherd glanced up at his handler to confirm that this was all right while he was on duty. When he saw that it was, his tail began to wag like crazy. He pressed against Liam and Becky, rubbing his head against Liam as playfully as a puppy.

Julie also gave the police dog a pat. "Max is so smart!" she said admiringly as they ran over to line up. "I bet he'll find that thief, no problem!"

"Of course he will!" Liam agreed as they joined the rest of the class.

"I just hope the thief's left some

chocolate for us to buy at recess!" Becky joked.

A slim, brown-haired woman was waiting for everyone to stop chattering and be still. It was Ms. Kendall, Becky and Liam's teacher. She gave a signal for the girl at the front of the line to lead everyone into their new classroom.

"Hello, Liam. Hello, Becky," she said, smiling as they passed. "I see Julie's already taking care of you," Ms. Kendall went on. "You can sit together in class if you like."

"Oh, Ms. Kendall, can Paul Carter sit with us as well?" Liam asked. "He's a new boy, too."

Ms. Kendall looked surprised. "Well, he's not in my class," she said. "You and Becky are my only new pupils this term."

"That's odd." Liam frowned as they filed into the classroom.

Becky looked just as puzzled.

"You must have made a mistake," said Ms. Kendall.

Chapter Five

"It's really *weird* about Paul, isn't it?" Liam remarked as he and Becky walked up to the front door of Lark Cottage. They'd just finished their first day at Ellandale Elementary, and all in all, it had been okay.

Becky nodded. "Sure is. How come he hasn't been registered at Ellandale Elementary if he's living here now?" She unlocked the front door and pushed it open. Then she laughed. "Hi, Max! You must have heard us coming, as usual!"

Max was waiting eagerly behind the front door, woofing a welcome and looking very pleased to see them. He pawed impatiently at the carpet until both Becky and Liam had dropped their schoolbags and begun to fuss over him.

"Dad must be home," Liam said as he rumpled Max's thick coat.

"No, he had to go to a meeting at another police station after he finished his shift," said Mrs. Wilson, coming out of the living room. "Hello, you two. How was your first day?"

"Okay," Liam and Becky said together.

Liam stuck his head inside the living room to see what his mom had been doing. He whistled. "Hey, Mom, this looks great!" The boxes had been unpacked, the curtains had been put up, and all the furniture was now in place — although when he tried to switch the TV on, he was disappointed to see that the picture wasn't clear.

He followed Becky into the kitchen, where their mother was in the middle of unpacking more boxes. The radio news was on.

"Police are becoming increasingly concerned for the safety of a young boy who disappeared from his home in Buxton two days ago. . . ."

Then the radio report was drowned out by a hopeful-sounding woof from Max. Liam turned to see his mother holding Max's leash. "Dad said you can take Max out for a walk if you like," she said.

Max sat, ears pricked at the word "walk," tail thump-thumping on the carpet. His warm brown gaze switched from one twin to the other, pleading for one of them to put his leash on.

"Actually, if you're taking Max out now, perhaps I'll go, too, and see Dr. Fenwick," Mrs. Wilson said. She reached out and turned off the radio. "I need to confirm which patients I'll be visiting when I start work." The twins' mother was the new district nurse for Ellandale and the surrounding area, but her job didn't start for a few more days. "We'll have a snack when you get back, okay?"

"Let's go the same way we went yesterday," Liam suggested as they began their walk. "We might meet Paul again."

Becky nodded. "Okay."

They went exactly the same route, letting Max have a good long run in the fields.

There was no sign of Paul.

But when they were about to head for home, Becky suddenly grabbed Liam's arm. "Look, there he is!"

Paul was wandering along the road in front of them. Liam yelled, "Paul! Wait!" as loudly as he could.

Paul glanced around, and seeing it was Liam and Becky, he stopped, though he didn't look particularly pleased to see them.

Liam thought Paul looked really tired — and a bit scruffy.

"Hi!" Becky said breezily. "We were hoping to see you. Why weren't you at school today?"

Paul blinked. "Oh . . . I . . . I couldn't come," he muttered.

"Why not?" Liam demanded.

"We're still unpacking and settling in," Paul replied. He shuffled his muddy sneakers. "I'll probably start next week."

"You're not on our class register, though," Liam argued, puzzled. And though he didn't say anything, he didn't think much of Paul's excuse for not starting school today like he and Becky had. After all, they'd just moved to Ellandale, too!

"Oh . . ." Paul cleared his throat. "The school must have made a mistake. Look, I've got to go home now."

"Maybe we could come with you," Becky suggested. "We could help you unpack, and we could meet Bouncer."

"No," Paul snapped — rather rudely, Becky thought. "We're going out shopping soon, so I've got to get home." And he ran off.

Liam nudged Becky. "Do you think we should go after him? Max can follow his scent!"

"No. Mom'll go crazy if we're late getting home," Becky said firmly.

"But there's definitely something odd going on," Liam grumbled.

"You're just nosy, that's all!" Becky grinned at him. "But maybe we should tell Dad about Paul."

"Right," Liam agreed.

They took Max home by a different route, going into the town instead of cutting through their backyard.

As they walked up the main street, they saw the police station on their left.

A balding, middle-aged man in uniform was standing by the bulletin board outside, taking down some of the old posters. He had a new rolled-up one under his arm.

Becky nudged Liam. "Hey, look. Do you think that's Sergeant Thornton?"

"There's only one way to find out," Liam replied.

The man glanced up as the twins and Max went over to him.

"Hello, are you Sergeant Thornton?" Becky asked.

The man nodded.

Becky beamed. "We're Liam and Becky Wilson. And you must have met Max."

"Oh, hello," Sergeant Thornton said gruffly. "Your dad's not here. He's gone to a meeting."

"Yes, we know," Liam said cheerfully. "We just thought we'd say hello."

Sergeant Thornton didn't look very impressed. He continued taking down the posters, frowning at Max as he did so.

"Don't you like dogs, Sergeant Thornton?" Liam asked.

Becky grinned to herself as Sergeant Thornton looked rather uncomfortable. Liam didn't have any problem with putting people on the spot!

"It seems to me we've managed well enough in Ellandale without a police dog in the past," Sergeant Thornton muttered, unrolling the poster under his arm.

Liam opened his mouth to argue, but Becky clutched his arm before he could speak.

"Liam!" she cried. "Look!"

The poster's headline read MISSING: HAVE YOU SEEN THIS BOY? And underneath it was a large photograph — of Paul.

Chapter Six

"Paul Carter disappeared from his home in Buxton two days ago," Becky read aloud. "Paul is ten years old and has brown hair and blue eyes. If anyone has any information about his current whereabouts, please contact your local police station immediately."

Sergeant Thornton had finished pinning the poster up and was heading back into the station. Liam, Becky, and Max raced after him.

"Sergeant Thornton!" Liam panted.

"What is it now?" Sergeant Thornton sighed crossly.

"That boy on the poster!" Liam gasped. "We've seen him!"

"Twice!" Becky added.

Sergeant Thornton stared at them suspiciously. "Are you sure?" he asked as a police car drove up to the station and came to a halt.

"Oh, look! It's Dad!" Becky cried, relieved. Their father would believe them. After all, he'd met Paul himself yesterday.

"What's going on here?" John Wilson asked as the twins and Max ran over to him, followed by Sergeant Thornton.

"Dad, that boy who's missing — it's Paul!" Becky said urgently.

"What?" Officer Wilson looked puzzled as he leaned over and said hello to

Max. "I'd heard that there was a boy missing, but I haven't seen any of the details yet."

"Look, Dad!" Liam pointed at the poster. "It's Paul!"

His father stared. "Good grief! That's the boy who came to lunch yesterday. I thought there was something odd about him!" He turned to Sergeant Thornton. "So what's the story, Jim?"

"Paul's parents reported him missing to the Buxton Police Station yesterday," Sergeant Thornton explained. "They think he must have sneaked out the night before because his bed hadn't been slept in."

"Any idea why he ran away?" Officer Wilson asked.

"His parents think it might be because of the family dog," Sergeant Thornton replied. "Apparently, they decided to take it to an animal shelter for adoption. They're both very busy people and found the dog to be too much work. It was pretty destructive around the house."

Liam looked at Becky.

"Bouncer!" he said. "Dad, Paul told us he had a dog, but he didn't say it had been given away!"

Officer Wilson looked at Liam and Becky. "When was the last time you two saw Paul?" he asked urgently.

"Just now," Liam explained. "When we took Max for a walk."

"You'd better take me to the exact spot," Officer Wilson said. He took Max's leash from Liam. "Max might be able to find him if it wasn't too long ago."

"There's a search party being organized for tonight," Jim Thornton added.

Liam and Becky glanced at each other. They knew that the police often conducted searches at night. There were fewer people around then, so there was more chance for police dogs to pick up the scent of the missing person.

Their father had explained to them before that when people like Paul were missing and feeling scared and alone, their body gave off scents that a highly trained police dog could pick up on.

"Okay, let's go." Officer Wilson hurried off, with Max trotting beside him.

"Imagine running away from home!" Becky shivered as they all went up the street. "I wonder where Paul's been sleeping?"

"In the fields, probably," Liam replied. "No wonder he looked so messy the last time we saw him."

They both fell silent as they ran to catch up with Max and their father.

"Paul might have moved on, of course," Officer Wilson said as they reached the road where the twins had seen Paul. "But if we're lucky, he might still be around this area." He released the German shepherd from his leash and said, "Max, find him!"

Max set off along the road, sniffing the air, his eyes bright and alert. Nothing distracted him while he concentrated on the search for the missing boy.

Officer Wilson, Liam, and Becky followed. They all searched until dusk began to fall, but there was no sign of the runaway boy.

After an hour or so, Officer Wilson gave up. "Come on, you two," he called. "We'd better get home. Your mom's going to be wondering where we are. There'll be a search party out tonight, anyway."

"Poor Paul." Becky shivered as they headed homeward. "It's getting chilly."

"Yes, we're in for a cold snap overnight." Officer Wilson looked worried. "Let's hope we find Paul before it's too late."

Chapter Seven

"PAUL!" Liam yelled at the top of his voice. "WHERE ARE YOU?"

"Stop, Liam!" Becky clapped her hands over her ears. "This isn't working!"

It was the following afternoon. The twins had just arrived home from school and had gone straight out into the countryside again to look for the missing boy. A search party, including Officer Wilson and Max, had been out searching the previous night, but they hadn't found any trace of Paul.

If Max hadn't managed to find anything, Becky didn't really see what she and Liam could do, but Liam was determined to try, and Becky had gone along with him, as usual.

"He's got to be here *somewhere*," Liam wailed, frustrated.

"Yes, but if he knows everyone's looking for him, he won't come out, will he?" Becky said sensibly.

Everyone at school had been talking about the missing boy earlier that day. Liam and Becky had asked lots of people if they'd seen Paul. But surprisingly, nobody had.

"Well, he must have found a good hiding place if *no one*'s seen him," Liam remarked. "But where?"

Becky glanced at her watch. "Look, we'd better go," she said. "Mom said to be home by six, and it's getting dark, anyway. I just hope Paul's safe and warm wherever he is," she sighed.

Liam nodded, but secretly he didn't think there was much chance of that.

When the twins arrived home, they were surprised to see that Sergeant Thornton was there, having a mug of tea in the kitchen with their parents.

"Has Paul turned up, Dad?" Liam asked hopefully.

"I'm afraid not," his father replied. "We did find evidence that someone had been camping out in a field at the back of our yard, but it looks as if the person has moved on. Perhaps it was Paul."

Max was lying under the kitchen table, one eye open and one closed. Liam noticed that Sergeant Thornton was keeping a wary eye on him as he slowly drank his tea.

"Did you find out any more about Paul's dog, Dad?" Becky asked.

Officer Wilson nodded. "Apparently, his parents were told by the animal shelter that Bouncer had been adopted in Ellandale."

"So *that's* why Paul came here!" Liam exclaimed. "Have you spoken to Bouncer's new owner, Dad?"

"Yes, her name is Mrs. Castle," Officer Wilson replied. "We interviewed her in case she'd seen Paul hanging around, but no luck — she hasn't."

"Did you see Bouncer?" Becky wanted to know.

"Yes, I did, and poor old Bouncer didn't look too happy, either!" Officer Wilson said, sighing. "I'd guess he's missing Paul just as much as Paul's missing him."

"So what happens now, Dad?" Liam asked.

"We've brought in some extra police officers for tonight, and we'll continue searching then," said their father. "Hopefully we'll find him before too long."

"Searching the countryside isn't easy," Sergeant Thornton said as he finished his tea. "If someone doesn't want to be found, there's not much you can do."

"Well, I'm sure Max will help." Officer Wilson leaned under the table and patted Max's flanks.

Sergeant Thornton sniffed. "I suppose dogs have their uses," he remarked shortly. "Some of the time, anyway." He stood up. "I've got to get going. Thanks for the tea, Mrs. Wilson," he said.

"He's a bit grumpy, isn't he?" Becky whispered as their mother showed Sergeant Thornton to the door. "And he doesn't seem to like animals much, either!"

Her father began to clear away the empty mugs. "I think he's just a bit set in his ways, that's all."

"Will you and Max still be coming to our assembly tomorrow, Dad?" Becky asked. "Or will you be too busy?"

"Oh, we'll come," her father replied. "It won't take very long, and besides, it's a good opportunity to ask if any of the pupils have seen Paul over the last few days."

"Oh, yeah — did you have any luck with finding the school thief, Dad?" Liam asked, suddenly remembering the events of the previous day.

Officer Wilson shook his head. "No, but this is far more important."

"I just can't stop thinking about that poor boy, out there on his own," Mrs. Wilson said, shaking her head as she came back into the kitchen. "It's just too hard to think about."

Chapter Eight

"Max is what we call a general purpose dog," Officer Wilson began. "He helps to track down criminals as well as find missing people and property."

Becky nudged Liam proudly as Max sat quietly next to their dad, not moving or making a sound. Officer Wilson had requested that his talk take place outside if possible, so there would be more chance of showing exactly what Max could do. All the classes were seated in rows on the playing field behind the school building. Luckily, it was a fine, warm day.

"Then there are other dogs who are trained to do specialist tasks," Officer Wilson went on. "Some look for explosives like bombs; others find illegal drugs. All our dogs begin with basic training, just like any dog might have." He quickly demonstrated how Max could sit, stay, walk, come to heel, and so on.

"The German shepherd is a good police dog for several reasons," Officer Wilson explained. "They have highly developed senses and keep a close eye on everything that's going on."

Everyone laughed as Mrs. Mason coughed and Max's ears pricked up.

Officer Wilson led Max away from the watching children, told him to sit on the grass, and then walked off. "I'm going to show you just how good Max's hearing is, but I'll need you to be quiet first!"

Everyone's so quiet, you could hear a pin drop, Liam thought with a grin. Max was certainly a hit with Ellandale Elementary!

"You can see that I'm now about 65 to 75 yards away from Max," Officer Wilson said. Then he lowered his voice to a soft whisper, which even the audience could hardly hear. "Down, Max."

Max immediately lay down on his stomach, dark eyes fixed on his handler.

"Stand," Officer Wilson whispered, and Max climbed to his feet. Everyone watched, hardly daring to breathe in case they distracted Max.

"Sit." At the next command, Max sat down again.

"That's called distance control." Offi-

cer Wilson smiled at the look of amaze-
ment on the children's faces. "And it
shows just how good Max's hearing is!"

The whole school applauded as Max
trotted patiently back to his handler.

"Now I'll show you some of the special things that Max can do." Officer
Wilson glanced at Liam and Becky's
teacher. "Ms. Kendall, do you think you
could help us out?"

The teacher looked surprised. "Certainly," she agreed.

"I'm going to walk Max to the other end of the field," Officer Wilson explained. "Could you go and hide around the corner of the school building, out of sight?"

He turned and led Max away at a brisk trot. Ms. Kendall hurried off the field toward the school. When the teacher was hidden, Officer Wilson brought Max back.

"This is how we find missing people or criminals," he told everyone. "Search and locate, Max!"

Max was immediately on full alert, every muscle tensed. He sniffed the air and then bounded forward heading away from the field and toward the school. As everyone craned their necks to see what was happening, Max stopped a little way from the corner of the building, and began to bark loudly.

"Well done, Max!" Officer Wilson called. "Okay, Ms. Kendall, you can come out now!"

"I'm glad I'm not a real criminal!" Ms. Kendall remarked thankfully as she rejoined her class.

Officer Wilson grinned. "Like I said before, Max doesn't just find people, he also locates property. Mrs. Mason, could I borrow your scarf, please?"

"Of course," the principal agreed. She untied the silky blue scarf from her neck and handed it over.

Officer Wilson took it partway across the field and hung it out of sight, on the branch of a large tree. "Now let's see if Max can find it!" he said.

Everyone watched intently as Max was sent off across the field to "find." Within a few seconds, he was heading for the tree. And as soon as he reached it, Max began to bark.

There was a gasp of admiration, and everyone clapped loudly. Liam and Becky joined in proudly. Max had done it again!

Officer Wilson explained that Max was trained to pick up the scent of humans in unexpected places. "But if there are lots of humans around, it can put a dog off from finding the scent of just one," he went on. "That is why I took the scarf across the field, away from all of you."

The trick was repeated several times, using another teacher's watch and then a small coin. Max found them all easily.

Afterward, everyone was invited to ask Officer Wilson questions. By the time all the questions had been answered, the bell rang for morning recess.

Mrs. Mason thanked Officer Wilson for coming. "But before you go off to play, Officer Wilson has something he would like to ask you," she added. "It's about Paul Carter, the boy who's missing."

Liam and Becky glanced at each other.

"Yes. I'm sure you've all seen the posters around town," Officer Wilson said. "Paul has been spotted near Ellandale, so if anyone else has seen him over the last couple of days, I'd be very interested to hear about it." He looked around as the children started muttering to one another, but no one put his or her hand up or said anything.

"Oh, well, maybe Paul will be found today, anyway," Liam sighed as each class stood up in turn and made its way into the playground.

"Let's hope so," Becky said quietly.

"My class next," called Ms. Kendall, who was on playground duty.

* * *

Toward the end of recess, Officer Wilson, who had popped into the teacher's lounge to have a quick cup of coffee, came out into the playground again with Max.

They were immediately mobbed. Everyone was eager to stroke the police dog, who took it all in stride.

Liam and Becky were dying to go and fuss over Max themselves but decided to let everyone else have a chance first. Then, when the bell rang and the others left to line up, they rushed over and gave Max a quick hug.

"You were great, Max!" Becky exclaimed.

Max was thrilled to see them. He swished his tail furiously from side to side, snuggling up against the twins as they both crouched down to hug him.

"You two had better go and line up," Officer Wilson said. "Max and I are going to join the search party now."

"Good luck!" said Liam, giving Max a final pat as he walked off with their father. Max wasn't taking much notice, however. He was already sniffing the air and looking around intently.

The twins ran over to join the end of

their class's line. But a short, sharp bark made them turn around. Max was showing great interest in an old, run-down shed that stood in a corner of the playground.

"Ms. Kendall, what's in that shed?" Officer Wilson called, looking puzzled.

"Well, nothing really," Ms. Kendall replied. Asking another teacher to keep an eye on the fourth graders as they went back into their classroom, Ms. Kendall hurried over to Officer Wilson. Liam and Becky followed, determined not to miss out on anything. "We don't use it much," the teacher added. "There's some old gym equipment in there, but that's all."

Max was now pawing at the shed door and barking.

Officer Wilson examined the lock.

"It's broken," he said. "I think I'd better take a look inside."

The twins held their breath as the door creaked open. They all peered in.

"Look!" Liam pointed at the floor. It was littered with chocolate wrappers, potato chip bags, and empty milk cartons.

Max was pulling his handler toward a dusty pile of gym equipment.

There was a scuffling sound from behind a pile of rickety-looking wooden benches, and then a boy appeared, blinking in the light.

"Paul!" Liam and Becky exclaimed together.

Chapter Nine

"I came to look for Bouncer," Paul muttered, in between mouthfuls of fish sticks, french fries, and peas. "That's why I ran away."

After Max's amazing discovery, things had moved fast. Officer Wilson had radioed the police station to let them know that Paul was safe and that the search could be called off. Then Paul's parents were called, and he was taken back to Lark Cottage for a meal while he waited for them to arrive.

He was sitting there now, with Max at

his side and the Wilsons listening to his story. Liam and Becky had pleaded to be allowed to go back to Lark Cottage with Paul. Because it was shortly before lunchtime, Mrs. Mason and Ms. Kendall had agreed — so long as they were back in time for afternoon classes. Now they were hanging onto Paul's every word.

"But why did your parents give Bouncer away?" Liam asked.

Paul's eyes filled with tears.

"Tell us what happened, Paul," Officer Wilson said gently.

Paul swallowed hard. "Well, we got Bouncer from an animal shelter," he began. "He's really great, and I love him. But he's very badly behaved. He chewed *everything*. And he kept wrecking the furniture and the carpets. Then the neighbors started to complain because he barked all the time, too."

"So your parents just got rid of him!" Liam exclaimed in disgust, then was quiet as both his parents gave him a warning look.

"They didn't want to," Paul explained sadly. "They loved Bouncer, too, but they said they couldn't cope."

Liam opened his mouth to say something else, but Becky nudged him and he closed it again.

"So we took Bouncer back to the animal shelter," Paul went on in a wobbly voice. "My mom asked them to let us know when they'd found him a good home. Then they told us that someone in Ellandale was going to adopt him."

"So you came here to try to find him," Officer Wilson said gently.

Paul nodded. "I caught the bus here four days ago, and I've been looking for him ever since. I just want to see him again." He bit his lip, struggling to hold back the tears now.

There was silence for a few moments. "I didn't think anyone would look for me in the school shed," Paul went on. "I hoped everyone would think I'd stay outside of town."

"You were right, Paul," Liam said. "And if it weren't for Max, you might still be there, miserable and hungry!"

Paul gave him a shaky smile and nodded. "I noticed the shed when I took the milk and stuff," he explained. Then he looked at Officer Wilson and blushed. "Honestly, I've never stolen anything before. But I was so hungry —"

"Don't worry about that now," the policeman said reassuringly. "I'm sure we can deal with it later."

Just then, there was the sound of a vehicle pulling up outside.

Paul turned pale. "That'll be Mom and Dad. They're going to be really mad at me — I know they are!"

"I wouldn't worry about that, either," Officer Wilson said. "I think they'll just be happy to see you safe and sound!"

Paul swallowed and nodded, although he still looked tense when Officer Wilson got up to open the door. At the same time, Max jumped to his feet and followed his handler, sniffing the air with interest.

"You should ask your mom and dad to let you have your dog back!" Liam said to Paul.

Paul shook his head. "I can't," he sighed. "And anyway, Bouncer's got a new home now."

"Ssh!" Becky said. "What's that?"

They all listened.

Max had bounded ahead to the front door and was snuffling and sniffing along the bottom of it with great interest. He gave a short, sharp bark. Then the sound of scrabbling and whining came from outside, along with an answering bark.

"Hey, there's another dog out there!" Liam began.

But Paul was already on his feet. "That's Bouncer!" he gasped.

Chapter Ten

As Officer Wilson opened the door, a shaggy brown tornado hurtled in. The little dog paused only to have a quick, friendly sniff at Max before racing down the hallway, barking loudly.

Paul was already running to meet him. "Bouncer!" he yelled. The dog leaped into his arms, yapping with delight. Paul didn't seem to know whether to laugh or cry. "What are you doing here?"

As Paul hugged Bouncer, two people rushed through the front door, pausing only to have a brief word with Officer Wilson.

Liam guessed that these were Paul's parents. But why did they have Bouncer with them?

"Paul!" Mrs. Carter's face lit up as she caught sight of her son. Both she and Mr. Carter were very pale, and their eyes looked as if they hadn't slept a wink for

the last few days. "We've been so worried about you!"

"Sorry, Mom," Paul muttered as both
his parents hugged him tightly. Liam and
Becky both beamed as they watched.
Meanwhile, Bouncer barked furiously,
and Max joined in occasionally.

"Let's all sit down, and I'll put the
teakettle on," said Tina Wilson with a
smile.

Tears in her eyes, Mrs. Carter flopped
into a chair. She still had an arm around
Paul, who was still holding Bouncer.

"Paul, if only you'd told us how much
you were missing Bouncer!" Mr. Carter
said. "We'd have gotten him back. You
shouldn't have just run off like that!"

"Sorry," Paul said guiltily.

"The thing is, we were missing him,

too!" Mr. Carter said. "Even though he *was* so naughty!"

Paul still looked dazed. "But, Mom, why is Bouncer here?" he asked. The little dog was trying to lick every inch of Paul's face.

"Well, we called the animal shelter this morning to see if there was any chance of us getting Bouncer back," Mrs. Carter explained. "And it turned out that Mrs. Castle, Bouncer's new owner, had called the shelter just a few hours before. She said Bouncer wasn't eating, and she was worried that he wasn't going to be happy with her."

"So Mrs. Castle let us have him back." Paul's father was smiling from ear to ear.

Paul's eyes opened wide. "You mean — Bouncer's ours again?"

"He certainly is!" Paul's mother agreed.

"Great!" Becky and Liam exclaimed together. Paul was too overjoyed to speak. He simply hugged Bouncer even tighter and buried his face in the dog's shaggy coat.

"You should send Bouncer to training classes to stop him from behaving badly," Liam suggested.

Mr. and Mrs. Carter looked at him and nodded.

"The animal shelter suggested that, too," Paul's father said. "Somehow, we never got around to doing it before. But now we certainly will!"

Paul finally found his voice again. "Oh, this is so great!" he exclaimed happily. He bent down to pat the German shepherd on the head. "Thank you, Max!"

On Saturday morning, a couple of days later, Max was off duty, so Becky and Liam took him for a walk through Ellandale.

Everything had worked out for the best. Paul and Bouncer had been reunited and were back home, and Max was now known around Ellandale as the dog who had found the missing boy. He had become a local celebrity.

"It was a good thing Max was on the case!" Liam said, ruffling the dog's thick fur. "If it hadn't been for him, Paul might have been missing for ages."

Becky wasn't listening. She nudged Liam. "Isn't that Sergeant Thornton?"

There was a row of stone cottages in front of them with small, flower-filled front yards. In the very end cottage the policeman was puttering around, dead-heading a clump of white rosebushes.

"That must be where he lives," Liam whispered back.

"Oh, good for you, Sherlock Holmes!" Becky grinned. "Let's go and say hello!"

"Why?" Liam wanted to know. "He doesn't like us much!"

"Yes, but he'll have to be nice to us now that Max is a hero!" Becky replied with a wink. "Hello, Sergeant Thornton!"

Sergeant Thornton certainly didn't look very pleased to see them. He gave them a grudging nod and carried on with his gardening.

"Everyone in Ellandale is talking about Max, you know, Sergeant Thornton!" Becky called. "He's going to be in the local newspaper, too!"

Sergeant Thornton managed a feeble smile. "*Is* he?" he muttered. "Well, I suppose he didn't do a bad job — for his first effort. Anyway, I'd better go in." And he turned and went toward the open door of his house.

"I suppose that's about as much praise as Max is going to get!" Becky said as they moved off.

"Oh, he'll change his mind when Max has solved lots more cases!" Liam said confidently.

"Inky! Inky! Come here!"

Liam and Becky stopped and looked at each other.

"That's Sergeant Thornton!" Becky whispered. "Who's he calling?"

They both peered through the hedge next door. Sergeant Thornton had come outside with a plate of food and was looking around the yard.

"Inky! Lunchtime!" he called.

As Liam and Becky watched, a huge, glossy black cat strolled out from behind a lavender bush. Yawning, it padded across the lawn toward the plate.

"Who's a pretty cat?" Sergeant Thornton murmured, stroking Inky as he began to eat.

Liam and Becky looked at each other, trying not to giggle.

"How about that!" Becky whispered. "He's just a big softie, really!"

Liam grinned. "I'm so glad we moved here," he said. "Living in Ellandale is going to be *great*, isn't it, Max?"

And Max wagged his tail and woofed in agreement.